For Jo, my sister

Brimming with creative inspiration, how-to projects, and useful information to enrich your everyday life, Quarto Knows is a favourite destination for those pursuing their interests and passions. Visit our site and dig deeper with our books into your area of interest: Quarto Creates, Quarto Cooks, Quarto Homes, Quarto Lives, Quarto Drives, Quarto Explores, Quarto Gifts, or Quarto Kids.

Text and illustrations © Victoria Turnbull 2019.
First published in 2019 by Frances Lincoln Children's Books, an imprint of The Quarto Group.
The Old Brewery, 6 Blundell Street, London N7 9BH, United Kingdom.
T (0)20 7700 6700 F (0)20 7700 8066 www.QuartoKnows.com
A catalogue record for this book is available from the British Library.
ISBN 978-1-78603-177-8
The illustrations were created with graphite and coloured pencil
Set in Bellota
Published by Rachel Williams
Designed by Zoë Tucker
Edited by Katie Cotton
Production by Kate O'Riordan and Jenny Cundill
Manufactured in Shenzhen, China PP012019

1 3 5 7 9 8 6 4 2

Victoria Turnbull

Cloud Forest

Frances Lincoln
Children's Books

Umpa's garden was filled
with flowers and fruit trees.
It was my favourite place.

Sometimes Umpa forgot to water the garden.
But the clouds remembered for him.

He showed me how to poke
the little seeds into the warm earth
with my fingers and we waited
for them to grow.

A story
will help,

Umpa
said.

Stories make
everything grow.

So he read to me
and I learned to
follow the words...

Through the garden gate,

over the treetops,

across the meadow...

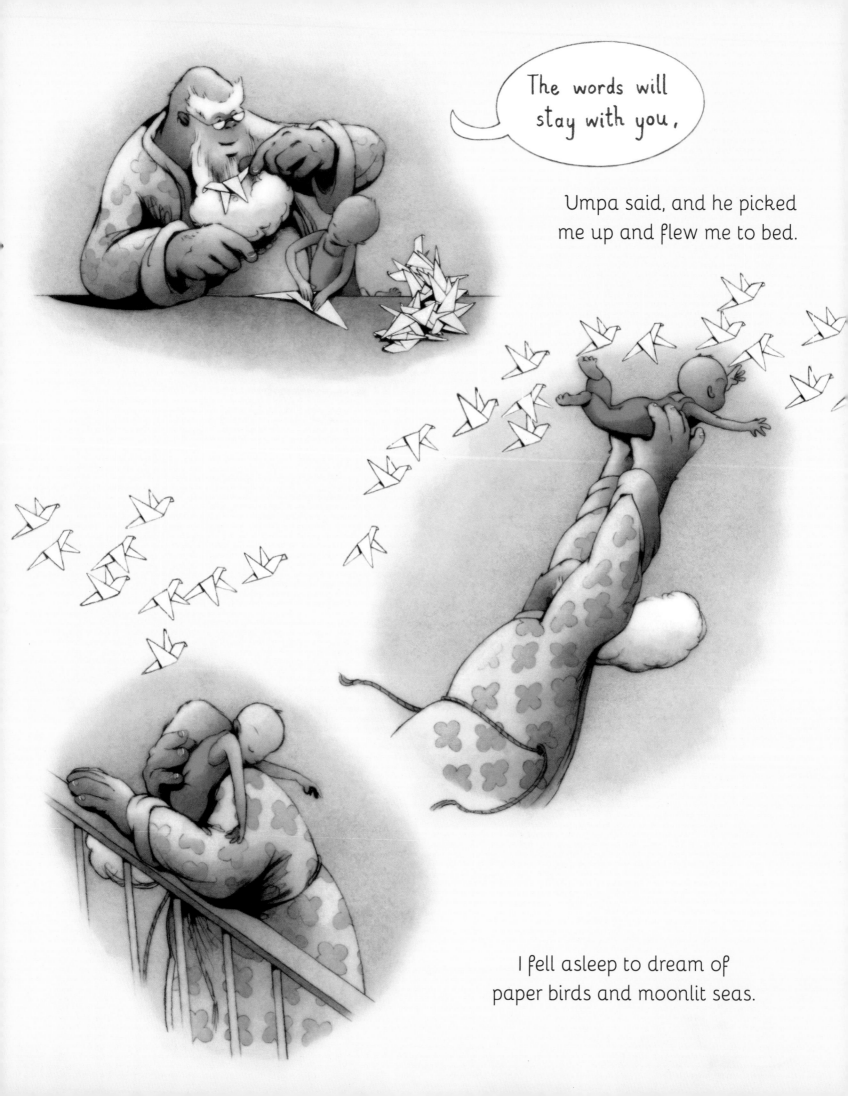

The words will stay with you,

Umpa said, and he picked me up and flew me to bed.

I fell asleep to dream of paper birds and moonlit seas.

That night the seeds began to grow.

As the first green shoots poked up through the earth,
we followed the words in search of castles in the sky.

When the rains came and
an ocean spilled from above,
Umpa gathered us up and
we sailed away to keep
our feet dry.

After the rains,
the sky was huge with stars.
The words sheltered us from monsters
that crept from the dark.

By Umpa's birthday,
the garden was in full bloom.
We feasted with friends until
the day was done.

The words made
our wishes come true.

Then Umpa was gone,
and he didn't come back.
For a time I hated
everything.

I no longer searched for
castles in the sky. Or dreamed of
paper birds and moonlit seas.
And I couldn't see the stars.
The clouds had swallowed
me whole.

Until one day,
I remembered what
Umpa had
left me.

A path of words to follow...

to him.

The GO-AWAY BIRD

Julia Donaldson

Catherine Rayner

MACMILLAN CHILDREN'S BOOKS

The Go-Away bird sat up in her nest,
With her fine grey wings and her fine grey crest.

A little green bird flew into the tree.
"I'm the Chit-Chat bird. Will you chat with me?
We can talk of the weather, and other things
Like the colour of eggs, and the aches in our wings."
But the Go-Away bird just shook her head
And what do you think she said?

"Go away! Go away! Go away!
I don't want to talk today.
You're much too chatty; you're oh so scatty.
Just the sound of you drives me batty,
So listen to what I say:

Go away!
Go away!
Go away!"

A little red bird flew into the tree.
"I'm the Peck-Peck bird. Will you eat with me?
There are juicy berries on every twig.
We can peck, peck, peck till we both grow big."

But the Go-Away bird just shook her head
And what do you think she said?

"Go away! Go away! Go away!
I don't want to eat today.
Your eyes are beady; you're much too greedy.
Just to look at you makes me seedy,
So listen to what I say:

Go away!
Go away!
Go away!"

A little blue bird flew up to the tree.
"I'm the Flip-Flap bird. Will you fly with me?
We can spread our wings; we can soar up high.
We can cartwheel all through the bright blue sky."

But the Go-Away bird just shook her head
And what do you think she said?

"Go away! Go away! Go away!
I don't want to fly today.
You're whirly and whizzy and much too busy.
Just the sight of you makes me dizzy,
So listen to what I say:

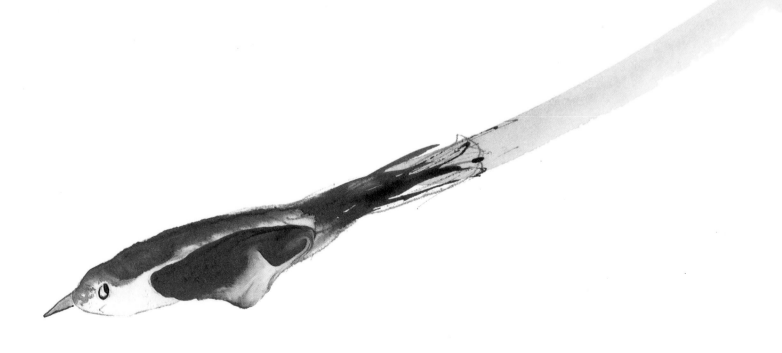

Go away!
Go away!
Go away!"

A brown bird hovered above the tree.
"Good day – I'm the Get-You bird," said he.
"I see I'm in for a special treat.
You're the very bird that I want to eat."

But the Go-Away bird just shook her head
And what do you think she said?

"Go away! Go away! Go away!
I don't want to be your prey.
I'm feeling wary; you're much too scary.
The situation is getting hairy,
So listen to what I say:

Go away!
Go away!
Go away!"

But the Get-You bird said,
"Now that I've met you,

I'm going to
get you,
get you,
get you!"

Then a yellow bird waddled towards the tree.
"Hello – I'm the Come-Back bird," said he.
He opened his bill and began to quack,

"Come back!
Come back!
Come back!
Come back!"

And back flew the others,

one,

two,   three,

All the way back to the tree!

And the five little birds all rose together –
A noisy mob of fluff and feather,
Red, blue, yellow, and green and grey –

And they chased that brown bird far away.

Then the Go-Away bird
hung down her head

And what do you
think she said?

"You can stay! You can stay! You can stay!
I do want some friends today.
Let's start playing – no delaying!
Let's get hopping and hip-hooraying.
Nobody go away!

YOU CAN STAY!
YOU CAN STAY!
YOU CAN STAY!"

For Gaia
JD

For Sandy
CR

JULIA DONALDSON has written some of the world's best-loved children's books, including *The Gruffalo* and the What the Ladybird Heard adventures. She was Children's Laureate 2011-13 and has a CBE for Services to Literature. Julia and her husband Malcolm divide their time between West Sussex and Edinburgh, and love to travel. Julia was very happy to hear the Go-Away bird's call for herself on a trip to South Africa, but is less keen to meet a hungry Get-You bird.

CATHERINE RAYNER is an award-winning author and illustrator. She studied Illustration at Edinburgh College of Art, and still lives in the city with her husband and two sons. Catherine was named as one of BookTrust's ten Best New Illustrators in 2008, and in 2009 she won the prestigious CILIP Kate Greenaway Medal. Catherine loves animals and has a horse, a cat and a goldfish which all inspire her work but, so far, no birds.

THE GO-AWAY BIRD is a real bird that lives in Africa. It has smoky grey feathers, a long tail and a crest on its head that can be raised up when the bird is excited. The Go-Away bird makes its nest from thin, often thorny twigs. It is named after its call, which sounds as if it is shouting 'Go away!'. But in spite of this, Go-Away birds can sometimes be found in groups of up to 20 or even 30 – so perhaps it is quite friendly after all!

First published 2019 by Macmillan Children's Books
an imprint of Pan Macmillan, 20 New Wharf Road, London N1 9RR
Associated companies throughout the world
www.panmacmillan.com

ISBN: 978-1-5098-4358-9

Text copyright © Julia Donaldson 2019
Illustrations copyright © Catherine Rayner 2019

3 5 7 9 8 6 4

A CIP catalogue record for this book is available
from the British Library.

Printed in Spain.